Praise for
KRISTINE KATHRYN RUSCH'S
DIVING UNIVERSE

"The Diving Universe, conceived by Hugo-Award winning author Kristine [Kathryn] Rusch is a refreshingly new and fleshed out realm of sci-fi action and adventure."
—*Astroguyz*

"Kristine Kathryn Rusch is best known for her Retrieval Artist series, so maybe you've missed her Diving Universe series. If so, it's high time to remedy that oversight."
—*Analog*

"As I frequently say, of Rusch's stories, they are enormously entertaining and I can't wait for the next one."
—*SFRevu*

"...a story of exploration of an artifact on an alien world, a bit reminiscent of the sort of story that Jack McDevitt writes."
—*Eyrie* on *The Spires of Denon*

"*Escaping Amnthra* is a full-fledged action adventure filled with high stakes and near-death experiences."
—*Realms & Robots*

The Diving Universe
(Reading Order)

MAELSTROM

A DIVING UNIVERSE NOVELLA

KRISTINE KATHRYN RUSCH

*wmg*PUBLISHING

Maelstrom

Copyright © 2021 by Kristine Kathryn Rusch

All rights reserved

Published 2021 by WMG Publishing
www.wmgpublishing.com
First published in *Asimov's SF Magazine,* Sept/Oct 2020
Cover art copyright © Philcold
Book and cover design copyright © 2021 by WMG Publishing
Cover design by Allyson Longueira/WMG Publishing
ISBN-13: 978-1-56146-374-9
ISBN-10: 1-56146-374-4

MAELSTROM

A DIVING UNIVERSE NOVELLA

Maelstrom: The Final Voyage of the Gabriella
By
Nedda Ferguson-Lithe

Author's Note

RECREATING THE LAST DAYS OF A LOST SHIP PROVED A difficult writing challenge for me. I had already chosen an older form of storytelling as my medium, because I believed—and still believe—that this form suits my purposes best.

But I also need to maintain my journalistic standards, for my sake as well as the sake of the story. Many others have told tales of lost ships over hundreds of years, and those storytellers have all chosen to fictionalize certain parts of the narrative, if not the entire narrative.

My training will not allow me to do that.

Besides, that's not why I wrote this. I wrote this to find answers, sometimes to questions I hadn't even realized that I had. My need to know comes from a personal place. I lost my father on the *Gabriella*. I needed to know what, exactly, happened to him. I did not learn that. Not exactly.

But I learned more than I had known before.

I have spent years researching, interviewing, and organizing the information into something that resembles a narrative. We will never know what those final days were like for the crew of the *Gabriella*, but we have enough information to make an educated guess.

Which is what this is.

1

ONE-HUNDRED-AND-FIFTY YEARS AGO, BEFORE PLANS for the star port on Ius Prime were finalized, ships launched out of Ciudad Orilla on the northern-most edge of Yaguni. One of those ships, the *Maria Segunda*, took off on a Monday to explore the rim of the deepest crater on Ius Prime's largest moon.

The early inhabitants of Ius Prime named the moon Madreperla because of its luminescent qualities. Even in Ius Prime's intense daylight, the moon glowed.

Rumors floating around Ciudad Orilla promised vast stores of untold wealth inside that crater on Madreperla, from sea creatures with bones made of the finest glass to minerals needed for every single engine. The water that filled part of the crater, the stories went, contained healing properties, and had more nutrients than anything that humans had concocted thus far.

The *Maria Segunda*, a ship that had land-to-sea-to-space capabilities, set out to learn which of those rumors had a basis in fact.

She arrived on the rim on a Thursday, set down on what her crew thought was an ice shelf, and by Friday morning, found herself in the midst of what the crew later described as an ice storm.

Only it was unlike any storm they had ever seen. A massive wind swirled around them, and they were caught in the center of it. But that didn't stop ice pellets, rock, and other materials that seemed harder than rock from hitting the outside of the ship. The *Maria Segunda* had defensive shields but they were rotating shields, built to stave off laser weapons. The normal heat and weather shields that any space-to-land ship had were not up to dealing with this particular anomaly, whatever the heck it was.

In the space of an hour, the damage to the ship's exterior was so severe that there was a good chance the ship might not make it out of the relatively weak atmosphere of Madreperla.

The captain, Angela Nájar, ordered the mission abandoned, and then the ship started the lengthy process of attempting to launch in the middle of that storm. The ice shelf—or whatever it had been—collapsed as they fired their engines—and in that moment, the crew learned that the water, which all reports had said filled only part of the crater, was suddenly lapping at the rim.

The ship managed to hover, but couldn't get purchase on anything for a ground-to-orbit launch. Fortunately, Captain Nájar had piloted the *Maria Segunda* for nearly a decade, and knew how to handle a water launch.

She shifted the controls from ground to orbit to water to air, and somehow managed to get the *Maria Segunda* away from that rim. The ship also activated its distress beacon as it headed off the planet, a move that saved the crew.

The storm extended from the crater to the outer edges of the moon's narrow atmosphere. No matter what the crew tried, the *Maria Segunda* could not get away from the ice, rock, and whatever else pounded the exterior of the ship. The storm itself exerted force on the ship, trying to draw it inside the crater, so the *Maria Segunda*'s engines worked twice as hard as normal.

The ship's sensors went down first, followed by its defensive shields. Thankfully, the heat shield held until the ship reached space.

The *Maria Segunda* limped into orbit, its ability to communicate gone, its hull compromised in all but a few places, its engine damaged, and its crew demoralized. They huddled in the interior storage areas, all except Captain Nájar and her first officer Asima Chandy, who remained on the bridge, attempting to repair what bits of the ship they could using what few resources they had.

Fifteen hours later, the rescue ships arrived, too late for Captain Nájar and First Officer Chandy. The bridge had caved in on itself, and Captain Nájar and First Officer Chandy had tumbled into space. Their environmental suits should have held twenty-four hours of oxygen, but they did not. A later examination showed that the suits, stored in a cupboard on the bridge, had been damaged in the storm. The suits had provided little protection against the cold emptiness that Captain Nájar and First Officer Chandy found themselves in.

The rest of the crew survived, as did all of the ship's logs. The destruction of the *Maria Segunda* provided the founding brick of information about the mysterious "weather" surrounding what came to be known as Nájar Crater.

Other ships, attempting to mine the rumored vast riches of the crater, also experienced these storms, but none as severe as that which enveloped the *Maria Segunda*.

Scholars believe that the *Maria Segunda* received the brunt of some kind of weather system on Madreperla that somehow caused the hail of debris that ended up compromising the ship, and ultimately destroying her.

These storms are called maelstroms because there was nothing else like them anywhere in this sector of space.

No scientist has gotten close enough to study the maelstroms in depth. Any probe sent into a maelstrom gets destroyed within seconds.

Some scientists believe maelstroms are caused by interactions between the engines of any kind of ship and the strange materials inside the crater.

But other scientists dispute that. They note that the ships that got caught in maelstroms were all different, powered by different kinds of engines, and of differing sizes and strengths. There really isn't enough information to uphold any theory on the maelstroms.

But a maelstrom has a powerful effect on those who experience it.

The survivors of the *Maria Segunda*, to a person, quit working exploration vessels. All but five of them quit working in space altogether. The rest returned to a more regulated and crowded area of the local solar system, preferring to work at lower-level jobs or running schools to train others in space exploration, rather than exploring anything themselves.

Most spacers of the previous century believed what happened to the *Maria Segunda* was simply bad luck. Ships encounter bad luck all the time, and not all ships survive it.

Spacers of this century know differently. The region around Nájar Crater is one of the most dangerous in this sector. Space Traffic Control at Ochoa Star Port requires special waivers for anyone traveling to Madreperla, and even more waivers from anyone traveling to Nájar Crater.

Essentially the waivers give the rescue units from Ochoa Star Port the legal cover to decide whether or not to attempt a rescue of any ship that has traveled to the Madreperla.

People die on that moon.

But the lure of riches, some of them proven to exist, still tempt ships, ship captains, and crews to that moon, and that crater.

The lure of riches and the promise of adventure.

2

NORMALLY, BUSINESS AT THE ELIZABETA PUB ON A Sunday afternoon is spotty. Too far away from the chartered and cruise ship levels on Ochoa Star Port to receive an influx of arriving and departing passengers, too deep in the recesses of one of the commercial decks to attract an exclusive crowd, the Elizabeta appeals to the crews of working ships, or to the locals who need a drink before heading to the residential wing of the port.

The Elizabeta is small and dark, with low ceilings and no pretense at grandeur. Unlike most pubs on the Ochoa Star Port that lack a view, the Elizabeta doesn't try to recreate one. The walls are brownish black, mostly, although a large oval on the back wall is a rather sickly gray. The wall's surface leading down the narrow corridor to the restroom is peeling; long strips of material, curling like bits of shaved chocolate, hang at eye level, promising more damage as time progresses.

The area doesn't smell like chocolate, though; the environmental system there malfunctions enough that the regulars don't even notice—except one or two who took it upon themselves to routinely report the problem to the pub's owner Beta Linde, usually in stark and humorous terms:

The walls farted again, Beta.

or

For the sake of all that's sane, Beta, what'll it take for you to get rid of the smell of poo?

Beta Linde is immune to it all—the peeling walls, the gray patch, the bathroom stench. She's a second-generation pub owner, and likes to joke that she was raised on the rails beneath the bar, and learned how to mix a drink before she could walk.

Not that she mixes many drinks. The clientele of the Elizabeta drinks the alcohol made locally, everything from strong ales to equally strong (or stronger) whisky. No fruit juices are added to get rid of the bitter alcoholic bite that every type of alcohol brewed (or curated) on the port seems to have.

Some of the other bars specialize in exotic drinks, mixing the local alcohol with coffees or something caffeinated. And a handful of the bars, closer to the tourist decks, serve imported alcohol, which is usually smoother and easier to drink.

But the clientele of the Elizabeta doesn't need help drinking, and it doesn't seem like they're in the pub to cater to any refined taste. They're in the pub for camaraderie and, let's face it, to get drunk in a safe space where no one will take advantage of them.

Beta is a big woman, more muscle than fat, and often gets mistaken for a man when her back is turned. In the decades she's run the pub, her hair has gone from black to grayish black, just like the walls. Her skin has a leathery quality that is reminiscent of the whisky she serves. Amber in good light, muddy brown in bad.

She took over the pub from her parents when she was just twenty-five. Her parents decided to travel after years of listening to others talk about faraway places. Beta hasn't heard from her parents since. If anyone dares ask her about them, she shrugs and says she assumes they're dead.

Beta is the one who built the business, one customer at a time.

She did so by chucking out the tourists and letting the locals have a private space, one where they can discuss anything.

They often do. They're in each other's business, even though they pretend not to be. And Beta knows more about her regulars than she's willing to admit.

Or than she *was* willing to admit, before the loss of the *Gabriella*.

That final Sunday—July 15, 0099, by the Old Spacer's calendar, Midsummer 15 495, by Ciudad Orilla's calendar, and *you know, that day before the* Gabriella *left* by the pub's calendar—the Elizabeta has a distracted air.

Beta claims all days prelaunch are like that. Families hanging around the edges, crews preoccupied, and drinks flowing. Perhaps so, but some locals claimed this was worse.

The Elizabeta does not keep security footage—then or now—and the pub itself is a camera-free zone, so there are no recordings of the interior. The lack of visual documentation frustrates the legal system and makes Beta's private (but illegal) security possible.

So what follows here is this: direct quotes come from interviews with me, paraphrased dialogue recounted from memory appears as italics, and the rest (usually a consensus opinion) appears as part of the narrative. These minute (but important) distinctions are one of the many reasons I have chosen to tell this story in writing, rather than in the other media available to me.

That afternoon, every member of the *Gabriella's* crew walks through the Elizabeta. Some stop to drink. Others pay their tab in person, a spacer way of saying goodbye without the bad luck of speaking the words.

In the corner, near the stench and the gray patch, Corey Burfet and Belinda Pete huddle over ale and chips, arguing about money. He's a thin, small man, barely five-five and underweight, not intimidated by zero-g or by malfunctioning equipment. She's a large redhead, with tired eyes, and appears, to outsiders, to be the stronger of the two.

"He wanted to stay," Belinda says about that conversation. "He didn't like the idea of exploring the crater. But the job paid ten times more than usual, with half up front. I was the one who pushed him to go. I actually said you've been in tough situations before, and survived. What makes this one so different?"

He looks at her, lips thin, frown on his forehead. She has the sense he wants to argue with her, but doesn't. Spacers like Corey aren't the most articulate people. He worked alone in ship maintenance, babying the equipment that should repair itself but never really does.

Belinda's right; he has survived awful situations, and mostly they've become the stuff of self-indulgent legends: the time he rebooted an entire environmental system on a cargo ship at the very last minute; the time he shared a tank of oxygen with a co-worker he hated to keep them both alive; the time the gravity in his boots failed, and he spiraled into space, only to have a crewmember literally throw him a lifeline.

But the one Belinda is thinking of, the one she and Corey have only discussed once, is one he rarely talks about.

Corey was a junior midshipman on a cargo ship heading to the outer reaches of the sector, remote areas known only in stories of a lost civilization. *The Desert Bloom* had picked up 17-gallon drums of something—Corey never said what that something was (if he knew) and my research never turned it up either—and that something got stored in the smaller cargo bay below the bridge.

That was a flaw in *The Desert Bloom*'s design, albeit not an uncommon one. Regulation for cargo ships is spotty. Most of the regulation dealing with cargo ships concerns their cargo, not their design, unlike commercial ships and passenger vehicles, where safety of the inhabitants is as is important as an efficient use of internal space.

The cargo in that ship was most likely unregulated. Belinda does not know, and neither do the transport authorities, who have incomplete records of the incident.

Belinda knows only what Corey told her: that he nearly died on that trip, and he had the scars to prove it.

The incomplete records tell a similar story. Two days after picking up those 17-gallon drums of something, *The Desert Bloom* suffered a series of rolling explosions. The first happened in the center of that cargo bay, right in the middle of all the 17-gallon drums.

Corey was three cargo bays over, moving equipment and supplies out of the way to make room for the next cargo pickup. *The Desert Bloom* rocked in a way that never happened on ships—at least in his experience.

His cargo bay was doubly reinforced since *The Desert Bloom* occasionally trafficked in weapons. Corey never worked on those runs because they scared him. *The Desert Bloom* usually kept the weapons systems on the exterior bays, so they could be easily jettisoned if someone detected a problem.

Because of the double reinforcement, Corey didn't hear the first explosion or the second or the third. Only when *The Desert Bloom* rocked yet again, and the warning sirens flared, along with the automated announcement for all crew members to don environmental suits did he know something was very, very wrong.

Corey already had his suit on, as did two other crew members working beside him. They had been instructed to illegally dump any materials that either hadn't sold from previous runs or hadn't been un-loaded, so they were already handling materials that could be dangerous.

The rumbling of the next rolling explosion reached them, along with black smoke coming out of the environmental system into the cargo bay. Then *The Desert Bloom*'s environmental system abruptly shut off.

Corey felt an unnatural calm. He told investigators that calm saved him and the two crew members he was working with. He instructed them to activate the only escape pod inside that cargo bay as he opened the bay door.

The two crew members climbed into the pod. He was heading toward them when the walls around him exploded.

The explosion was so severe it shredded the back of his suit, injuring him. He could still move, and he pushed himself to the pod, barely catching it. The two crew members pulled him inside, sealed it, and set it to flee *The Desert Bloom* as quickly as possible.

The dry details sound orderly, but Belinda says what really happened was not. Corey would scream *Let me in, you bastards!* in his sleep and once, she says, he shouted, *I know how to destroy this thing's alert beacon. No one will find you!* When he woke after that, she didn't tell him what he said, but did get him to confirm that he had been having a nightmare about the destruction of *The Desert Bloom*.

The three people in that pod were the only survivors of *The Desert Bloom*. The ship's destruction, recorded by nearly a dozen ships in the area, show explosion after explosion, finally igniting something on the outer edge of the ship, and engulfing it all in white light, before it broke apart, sending bits of itself all over the cargo route.

The pod got picked up within the hour by another cargo ship, which immediately took Corey to the nearest star base, where he underwent medical treatment for his injuries.

The scars were deep, but he couldn't afford to have them removed. The nightmares were deeper and, Belinda says, often caused him to lash out in his sleep.

Corey wanted nothing more than to stop working on spaceships. He'd moved from cargo vessels to maintenance vessels to exploration ships. He thought exploration was the safest job he could find, but he learned it was dangerous in a completely different way.

His instincts told him to avoid the *Gabriella*. His finances told him to take the work.

His finances won, to Belinda's eternal regret.

She blames herself for his death, saying he would be alive now if he hadn't listened to her.

But Beta tells a different story. Beta knew Corey longer than Belinda did, and Beta says that Corey had this discussion before every mission.

"He wanted to get land-based work, or so he said." Beta shrugged as she recounted this. "But he never looked for any land-based jobs, and when he had money, he spent it. He didn't use it to pay for retraining or to move somewhere on Ius Prime. He was all talk. He knew the money was in space, not on land. And he couldn't really figure out a way around that."

3

Corey Burfet is not the only crew member having second thoughts about this trip. At least six others express concern to Beta—six who normally seem excited before a launch. The regulars who always whine are unusually silent.

A seventh, Imelda Fleites, quits hours before launch.

Imelda, a researcher who specializes in the unknown, the new, the strange, has never walked away from a job before, especially before the work starts. She even shows up at the Elizabeta for the day-before drinks and goodbyes.

She is tiny, white-haired, and forceful. An animated speaker, she jokes that her hand gestures can be lethal to anyone who sits near her.

She buys herself a whisky and sits in her usual spot at the bar. The conversation washes over her—typical pre-launch conversations about money with the family (*I made sure you have enough to survive the six weeks we'll be gone*), about the risks (*I hate thinking about potential problems just before we leave*), and about luck (*It's bad luck to say goodbye. Just wave, honey. Just wave*).

Usually, the conversations wash over her because they don't concern her. She has an on-again, off-again boyfriend who has his own funds, a family whose space-faring ways go back six generations, and an apartment that she owns free and clear in the residential wing.

She likes the work, likes seeing things no one else has seen, likes figuring out what she's looking at. But that day, she twists the whisky glass in her hand, without taking a sip.

"My stomach hurt," she told me. "The closer launch day came, the more my entire body tensed. I had done what research I could on Nájar Crater. Usually research like that excites me. I end up with long lists of areas I want explored, questions I want answered. I started out with a long list for Nájar Crater, but the more I investigated, the more stressed I got. It wasn't just the number of deaths associated with the crater, although that was a factor. It was the maelstroms. It wasn't that they were unpredictable. It was that they seemed inevitable—or, contrary to what others seem to think, extremely predictable."

A week before, she asked for a meeting with the ship's captain, Giles Ferguson, and discussed her hesitations. He seemed buoyed by her discoveries, saying she had already learned more than all the researchers before her combined.

"I told him I didn't like the maelstroms," she said. "Predictability in weather or in natural phenomenon isn't in *when* the phenomenon will appear. Predictability comes when certain meteorological or other factors come together to form the phenomenon. When we see those factors, we know that the phenomenon will form. But the predictability we're seeing here is something else entirely. If I didn't know better, I would say that what we were seeing had a human cause, not a natural one."

According to Imelda, Ferguson did not know the difference nor did he care. He said the trip wasn't about the cause of the phenomenon. It was to see if the riches inside the crater actually existed.

"Sometimes I think I should have tried harder to make him understand," she said. "But then there are days that I know nothing I could have said would have changed his mind. He wasn't looking at just one trip, you know. He was planning to go back and forth to the crater for the next two years. For him, each payday would have been larger than the last."

He told her as much in one of their final conversations, and offered her more money to take this trip. He promised her a berth on each successive trip, *to keep the research consistent*, he said.

"It was the money that I kept coming back to as I sat at that bar. He was throwing a lot of money at me. Too much. And as I sat at that bar with the other conversations going on around me, I realized most of them focused on how the money from this trip would allow the spacers to finally find a land-based job, would pay off old debts and pay for an escape from this area altogether. That bothered me, and I remembered something I had learned about money as a young researcher."

When Imelda worked on a post-doc at Ius University, one of the most prestigious space research schools on Ius Prime, she had received a job offer from a big corporate science lab. The amount of money they offered for her along with her research had been six times the amount of any other job offer she had received.

She had told her advisor this, and he had given her a knowing smile. *Before you accept the job*, he told her, *why don't you research the company that's offering it?*

She did, and learned her first big lesson about scientific integrity. Many organizations offer too much money to excellent researchers to leverage the researchers' reputations to promote bad science. The result is already determined; the researcher has to cherry-pick the evidence to find a way to make that result credible.

"I boiled down that lesson into a simpler one," she said. "I decided that too much money equals too much risk of compromise, and I don't believe in compromise."

So, on that final Sunday, she slides her whisky back to Beta, and walks out of the bar in search of Ferguson. Imelda finds him sitting in an "outside" table along the so-called promenade.

Most commercial districts of star ports have several promenades. On the exclusive levels, the promenades are designed to make patrons think they're outside in some exotic natural environment, complete with expensive water features and fake sunlight.

On most levels, the promenades resemble city centers of faraway famous places, with some replicas of the cultural icons hovering nearby. Or, if the displays aren't permanent, there's a rotating spectacle of VR images that show the tourist highlights of the planet below.

But the promenade outside of the Elizabeta is nothing more than chairs and tables and some gambling booths. The ceiling is as brown as the walls which are as brown as the floors. There's nothing special or even "outside" here, just a place to be away from the bar's noise, while still receiving the bar's service.

Captain Giles Ferguson is sitting out there alone, his fingers wrapped around a stein of a particularly skunky local beer called Ragtop. He drinks nothing but Ragtop at the Elizabeta, but unlike some of his shipmates, he never had the beverage delivered in quantity to the ship.

He is a lanky man, taller than the average spacer, but just as thin. He wears his silver-gray hair close cropped when he is in port, and keeps his face clean-shaven. By the time he returns from a voyage, his hair will be thick and loose and wild, and he will have a beard to match. It is as if he lacks the time for proper grooming when he has to deal with a ship and her intricacies.

That afternoon, he wears a blue-and-red flannel shirt so old that it shines at the elbows and collar. He leaves the shirt untucked over a pair of black pants, and the only thing that identifies him as a spacer are his black gravity boots, which some spacers even wear on land.

A gold chain hangs from his right wrist, and a matching chain glints underneath his shirt. He will give those to me for safe keeping in the hours before the ship launches. They are, he will tell me, the only things of value among his personal effects.

Imelda plunks her whisky on the table across from him, straddles a chair, and places her elbows on either side of her drink.

My gut tells me this run is too dangerous, she says. *The money scares me.*

He gives her a patronizing smile. *The money is the best thing about the run.*

Yeah, she says, *that's what I'm afraid of.*

The conversation goes on in this vein for nearly forty-five minutes. They talk in circles. And finally, she can't take it anymore.

I'm sorry, she says. *But I am not going with you.*

I already paid you a boarding fee, he says.

I'm not repaying the fee, she says. *You can keep the research I've done. You told me it's better than anything you've ever seen.*

He stares at her for a long time. She thinks about that stare often, how his gray eyes assess her, the way his lips twist just a little. Sometimes she thinks he was going to argue with her, and sometimes she thinks he admired her conviction.

But, truth be told, she has no idea what was going through his mind at that moment.

You'll leave us without a senior researcher, he says.

Get another, she says.

You know it's too late for that, he says.

A senior researcher is a silly luxury, she says. *The bulk of the researcher's work happens before the ship leaves. You don't need me to consult. You're smart enough to figure it all out on your own.*

He shakes his head just a little. *I never thought I would live long enough to hear a senior researcher disparage her job like that.*

She knows he said that almost word for word, because his voice echoes through her head even now. She used to argue that senior researchers were the ones who kept ships alive, warning captains away from bad situations, reminding captains that other ships had done something similar and had suffered for that action.

She even made that argument to Ferguson years ago when he flirted with using the information in a computer system alone.

But the problem with a computer system, she told Ferguson more than once, is that it doesn't speak up when a situation goes from comfortable to bad in just a few hours. A computer system does as it's told, and that is the most dangerous thing about it.

Human beings are the ones who stop tragedies, because it's hard to shut a passionate human being up. A computer system can be shut off. It can be told not to impart information to a captain or a crew because that information might make the captain or crew nervous.

When Imelda told me this, I asked: "Do you think that's what happened on board the *Gabriella?* Do you think the crew shut off all the computerized warnings?"

Her expression changed, and she looked away from me. "I don't know what happened on board the *Gabriella*," she said curtly. "I wasn't there."

Then she ended our interview, and, despite the help she has given me, she has never discussed the *Gabriella* with me again.

4

Twenty-four hours after Imelda's conversation with Ferguson, the *Gabriella* launches with a full crew compliment. Somehow, Ferguson has found another senior researcher, a good one. Josué Palmet has served with distinction on more than a dozen vessels and is much more qualified than Imelda Fleites is.

He also has more debts than she does.

He says a cursory goodbye to his family, fully expecting to return in six weeks, and disappears into the *Gabriella*, as do fifty other souls, the minimum crew required to run a ship like the *Gabriella*.

The *Gabriella* is a refurbished military vessel that looks vaguely like an infinity symbol. Only two different engines rotate what would be the two empty centers of the symbol. From a distance, it looks like the *Gabriella* has a black infinity shaped exterior with a white ghostly fog filling those center holes. Upon closer examination, the edges of the engines appear, their motion so constant that it's impossible to see their actual shape.

The military no longer uses the infinity shape. It is too vulnerable, too confusing. Most of the ships of that design were scrapped, but several were sold to nonmilitary organizations for use in distance travel, the thinking being that if the ship did not engage in military exercises, its complicated design wouldn't be a handicap.

After its purchase, the *Gabriella* went through a series of retrofits, mostly to add further protections to the engines. Even though the engines seem vulnerable and open in the original design, they did have triple shielding, as well as a clear bubble case made of the most solid materials available at the time.

The first retrofit left the bubble case intact, and added extra casings. The second retrofit upgraded all of the shields on the ship, and the third added a tiny backup engine to the detachable bridge at one end of the infinity design.

Williams & Docket, the company that purchased the *Gabriella*, paid extra to keep the weapons system intact. Other retrofitted military vessels had their weaponry removed.

Technically, civilian ships shouldn't have weapons systems like that. In addition to paying extra for the systems, W&D probably followed the same procedure other companies did when getting a fully functional military vessel: they paid bribes within the regulatory agencies and the military itself.

The bribes are impossible to track down, but W&D did receive the same treatment that other companies, later convicted of bribing officials, received. Those companies kept the systems and were required to maintain those systems, using one particular certification arm of the Regional Government of Yaguni.

Certifications, issued by that arm, show that W&D complied with the standard maintenance of those weapons systems, but whether or not the certifications are based on actual inspections is impossible to know. Other companies convicted in that later bribery scandal sometimes had actual inspections, while others did not.

What we do know is this: The *Gabriella* complied with the inspections of her engines and her upgraded shields. The certifications she received on those were from a different branch of the Regional Government of Yaguni, as well as the star port itself.

According to those certifications, the shields were upgraded with each advancement in technology, something some experts believe to be unusual.

"You don't willy-nilly just upgrade things," Harrison Carter, ship systems manager for Chapel Distributing, told me one sun-drenched afternoon in Ciudad Orilla. "Some of these new systems, they aren't truly compatible with the technology in the older ships, no matter what the developers of those systems say. And with military ships, that goes double, since the military has its own tech and its own tech secrets."

Chapel Distributing owns three ships with the same infinity design as the *Gabriella*, but unlike W&D, Chapel Distributing has not continually upgraded the systems.

Carter wouldn't tell me if Chapel maintains the weapons systems on its ships, but he led me to believe they had the systems removed.

"Weapons systems cause too much trouble," he said. "Regular defensive systems are good enough for most ships. With strong shields and enough firepower to hold their ground until help arrives, most ships stay out of trouble."

Does he believe that the *Gabriella's* extra weapons and the continual upgrades contributed to her loss?

"Unless you've seen the logs of a ship that's gone down, you don't know what destroyed her," he said. "Speculation helps no one."

He was necessarily circumspect—Chapel Distributing was one of W&D's biggest rivals, and benefitted the most from W&D's dissolution two years after the *Gabriella* was destroyed. But he pointed me to various research studies about the retrofitting of the infinity ships.

I needed help with the technical readouts, and consulted with a variety of engineers and experts. They looked over the *Gabriella's* specs, and told me conflicting things: that she was off-balance because of the extra shields, that the weapons systems would leach poisons into the environmental systems of a ship of that design unless preventative measures were taken; that the detachable bridge could detach accidentally under stress. Those are just a few of the things that the engineers and experts told me, and are the only ones that even a few of them agreed on.

The rest of the problems those engineers and experts mentioned include a whole host of gloom-and-doom scenarios, all of which have come to pass on other ships, but none of which happened to the *Gabriella* before her launch on that fateful Monday afternoon.

"Whatever we tell you is complete and utter bullshit," LaTonya Eircolan, a decorated expert in ship design and sustainability who teaches at two separate universities on Ius Prime, told me. She was the only expert willing to say that the experts might be wrong.

She said, "Most ships owned by struggling companies do a lot of off-the-books maintenance at places that don't comply with Ochoa's regulations—or any regulations, really. We have no way of knowing if the *Gabriella* went through that kind of maintenance, but I would wager she did. It's pretty common, especially for ships that operate on a shoestring, like the *Gabriella*."

When W&D dissolved, its records and holdings became property of the courts based in Ciudad Orilla because of that city's proximity to the Ochoa Star Port. The records are, as Eircolan posited, woefully incomplete.

I brought what I could find to her, and she pointed out a list inside the logs labeled *Staff maintenance*, along with various dates.

"Staff maintenance means that the crew repaired systems, often on a journey, and those repairs were allowed to stand." She shook her head a little as she explained this, and her expression was sad. "Most well managed companies have outside agencies review in-transit repairs.

Crews don't always have access to the latest equipment or even to the right tools to affect a proper repair. It's best practices to have a ship examined after each long journey. I'd prefer a ship to be examined every single time a staff repair occurs, no matter how small, but that's costly and few companies do it."

She sighed, and added, "More lives would be saved if all ships just followed those simple rules."

She has spent much of the past few years arguing with regulatory agencies and the star port for just those changes. I had expected to hear some of that advocacy when she spoke to me, but I hadn't expected the sensitivity in her tone.

She is cognizant of the lives lost on the *Gabriella*, and, it seems, she mourns them.

I wonder how many deaths she has seen due to improper repairs and maintenance, but I did not ask her that question.

I am afraid of the answer.

The questions she did answer unnerve me enough.

"There is nothing in W&D's records that indicate any review of in-transit repairs, not just for the *Gabriella*, but for all of W&D's vessels." She spoke matter-of-factly, her sad expression remaining. "I wish I could tell you this is unusual, but it is not. Not for a company on the brink, like W&D was."

W&D is the source of my greatest consternation in writing this account. At first, I thought it a shell company, because of the monies it had promised the crew of the *Gabriella*. According to financial records, W&D did not have the funds to pay the crew the elevated salaries it had promised.

Yet, it paid the signing bonuses out of an account that took me half a year to track down. That account linked W&D to other corporations, some of whom vanished when W&D dissolved.

W&D's dissolution is one of the great difficulties of my investigation, hampered also by the deaths of two of the principals, Sari Docket Marberry, and Lochlyn Quartz. Their deaths, first ruled suicide, have been deemed suspicious, and the government of Ciudad Orilla has locked down all information pertaining to them until the deaths are resolved.

Enough evidence leaked out to posit third-party involvement, perhaps with an entity no longer allowed to do business in this part of the sector, but any chance for further clarification is not, at this point, possible.

W&D was not always a struggling company with shady business practices. For nearly three hundred years, it was considered the gold standard of the industry, sending ships all over the sector. Early explorers who arrived on Ius Prime traveled in W&D ships.

W&D mined Yaguni, finding the best places for colonies. Many of those colonies turned into flourishing cities, including Ciudad Orilla. The early government of Ciudad Orilla contained family members of the owners of W&D, and a lot of W&D money funded everything from arts centers to Prime University itself.

Even Ochoa Star Port has links to W&D, allowing W&D ships to operate out of the port without the proper licensing and restrictions, something W&D took advantage of as its financial fortunes floundered.

Initially, news organizations reported that the money for the *Gabriella's* trip to Nájar Crater came from W&D itself, and its desire to once again become one of the great exploration companies of the entire galaxy. But a deeper dive into W&D's finances shows that W&D did not have the money to finance a trip like this.

It received large payments for the use of the *Gabriella* with notations that lead me to believe that more payments would come with the *Gabriella's* continued success in exploring the rumored wealth of Nájar Crater.

Just like the crew members of the *Gabriella*, the *Gabriella* herself stood to make more and more money with each successive journey to the crater.

The owners of the *Gabriella* either did not demand an overhaul of the ship before she launched that fateful Monday or Giles Ferguson held them off.

Ferguson had captained the *Gabriella* for most of his adult life. He treated her as his own. Every time something went wrong on a journey, he retrofitted the ship to prevent something similar from happening again. He did some of the repairs himself.

He also hired the same crew over and over again, until they moved on for better pay or managed to be one of the few spacers to retire. Imelda Fleites had first served on the *Gabriella* nearly a decade before, also on an exploration run which, she tells me, held no surprises for anyone.

Whenever she was available, Ferguson tapped her, as he did several other crew members. She estimates, and Beta Linde agrees, that Ferguson had a rotating roster of 150 regulars who would venture out with him on any given mission, depending on the mission's needs and some vagaries that neither of them pretend to understand.

Ferguson himself is a bit of an enigma. Married twice, father of four, his inability to stop moving made him more of a visitor than a member of any family. He seemed to like it that way.

Even in his first marriage, which lasted seven years, he had his own apartment at the star port because he hated spending too much time on land. He had a prenuptial agreement with his second marriage—unusual for a man of modest means—which stipulated that he and his second wife maintain their own residences, and any children born of the marriage live with his wife.

They did not have children—his four children came from the first marriage—and the second lasted less than two years. Even though he proposed a third time, to Keiko Flores, she repeatedly turned him down, saying she had no interest in tying herself financially to a man who had proven unreliable twice before.

She was unable to extricate herself from emotional entanglements, however, and when she spoke to me about him, she had to excuse herself often to wipe away tears.

She did not spend any time before launch with him. That was their customary practice, because he wanted to focus on the upcoming journey. The last time she saw him was a week before the *Gabriella* left, and their interaction was more practical than romantic, preparing for the flight, the long separation, and yes, the influx of money.

He wanted to give her half of his signing bonus, but she turned him down. She is a well-respected professor of literature at Prime University, and her salary there more than covered her needs.

She repeated their long-standing tradition of keeping their funds separate, but he had smiled at her, and held out his hands to her.

If this works, Keiko, I'll be a wealthy man. I want to share that with you.

Share it with me when it happens, Giles, she told him. *Not before.*

He had no will, so what money he did have (which was not much), his apartment, and all of his holdings went into a standard escrow for those lost in space. After five years, his children petitioned for—and received—access to his estate.

Keiko is not bitter about this. She believes anything he had earned should have gone to his family. She sees herself as an interloper in his life. His children and his previous wives suffered from their relationships with him, she told me. Her time with him, she added with tears punctuating the words, was the best in her entire life.

She smiled at herself when she talked about the launch.

"I imagine it as a big sendoff, with sweeping music and fireworks and waving children, like you see in the old videos of the early launches from the port. And, yes, I do know it was nothing like that."

Nothing at all. The launch is as prosaic as all other launches. Most family members do not come because they cannot see anything.

Ochoa Star Port has a viewing area for the arrival of tourist ships, has none for the daily launches and arrivals of commercial vehicles. If a family member wants to see a ship off, the family member must petition to go to the pertinent bay, stand in a steel-gray corridor, and watch as the crew member heads through the bay doors.

Not all crew members go through bay doors. Many of them use maintenance entrances, sometimes because of the equipment they're carrying, and sometimes because those entrances are more convenient to certain parts of the residential wing.

Some senior crew members, like Ferguson himself, sleep onboard the night before launch, if they sleep at all.

"I spend the night before launch double-checking systems," says Naomi Ruhl, Captain of the *Angelina,* which also launched that day. "I have a great crew, but they are not responsible for every aspect of the ship. I am. I take that responsibility seriously. I know Giles did as well. He always thought of the *Gabriella* as his. I think he would have bought her if he could have saved the funds. But Giles was like most of us in this business. He had no idea how to hang onto money."

On that fateful day, *Gabriella* launches three minutes early. Launch times at a star port like Ochoa are fluid things, based not just on what traffic control says, but also on when the crew arrives.

Star port records show that all 51 crew members arrived three hours before launch. The *Gabriella* ran through standard launch protocols, not waving any of them. Ferguson does not file a travel plan, but that's not required at Ochoa, the way it is at many other ports. Nor does he have to state the nature of the mission.

Because the *Gabriella* always docks at Ochoa, the ship does not have to follow the star port's strictest regulations. As is the case for most small commercial vessels that regularly operate through the port, what the ship does on its routine trips does not interest the authorities.

But this is not a routine trip for the *Gabriella*. When she has gone on exploration journeys in the past, she has traveled with half a dozen other ships, and they spend their time mapping the outer edges of known space. The methods they use are time-honored and somewhat old-fashioned.

Those ships explore regions of space that have been thoroughly mapped with long-range scanners. The ships' journeys are as much about scanner calibration as they are about discovering something strange and new and different.

The *Gabriella's* mission this time has nothing to do with strange and new and different. It is supposed to confirm the rumors that have long haunted Nájar Crater.

The *Gabriella* is not the first ship to undertake such a mission, and unfortunately, she is not the last.

5

NÁJAR CRATER IS THE LARGEST CRATER ON MADREPERLA.
Indeed, Nájar Crater is one of the largest craters in the
solar system. For centuries, scientists have assumed that
Nájar Crater is an impact crater, that something hurtling
at a great deal of speed hit the ground with an incredible
amount of force.

But geologists and others question that idea. The
presence of a mountain range around the gigantic hole
in the ground suggests that the crater might have been
formed during a volcanic eruption or several eruptions.

The rock around the crater isn't lava rock as we know
it, and there seems to be no volcanic activity on Madreperla. Some believe there never was volcanic activity.

It should be easy enough to study, those geologists tell
me, if only a ship could land nearby. But every time a ship
tries, a maelstrom comes, sometimes small, sometimes large.

Scans provide the basis for the theories, and scans
are a bit inconclusive. There are blind spots around the
crater, depending on where the scanning equipment is.

From equipment based on Ius Prime, the scans can't read the crater at all. The mountain range seems to be one long series of mountains, with a slight valley where the crater actually is.

That reading remains for ships outside Madreperla's orbit. But once ships enter Madreperla's orbit, they can scan and map the mountains and the exterior of the crater itself.

Those scans show a crater that's at least 10 miles deep and 500 miles wide. There is a bit of a flat area all the way around the crater, and then the ground rises up, forming the various mountains, all of which are incredibly steep and pointed. Young mountains, the geologists guess, although they're unable to get close enough to study them, either.

Ships that venture into the large area above the crater have started scans, which is how we know about the water, about the minerals, about the possibility of riches.

But those ships have been unable to complete their scans. A few of the ships dropped probes into the water, and that always starts a reaction. The probes do get some readings, however, and those readings are also woefully incomplete.

The water seems denser than we expect, and in addition to its mineral content, has the kind of natural nutritional content that most ships usually add to their own water supply artificially. The kind of content that keeps an entire crew of a starship healthy on a very long voyage.

The probes send back information until the maelstrom starts, and then the probes cease to communicate. None seems to make it more than a quarter mile down, although one started pinging the depth of the crater the moment the probe hit the water, and that's where we get the depth measurement.

That probe was getting readings that suggested the area it was pinging was 10 miles deep. But that doesn't preclude deeper areas in other parts of the crater, or shallower areas there as well.

"Sometimes I believe the only reason we're interested in the Nájar Crater is because we can't easily get information about it," says Lev Kevershaw, an astrogeologist who has spent his entire career at Prime University studying anomalies in this sector. "We usually have too much information. With Nájar Crater, we have just enough to be tantalizing, but not enough for us to make any conclusive determinations about what it is, what caused it or why it's there. And then there are the storms, if you want to call them that."

Storms is not a word that most scientists use lightly. Storms are natural phenomena that occur because of atmospheric conditions unique to a particular planet or moon.

No other location on Madreperla has this kind of activity. And, as Imelda pointed out, these storms are predictable. Every single dropped probe caused a maelstrom. Every single ship that got too close to the crater itself got enveloped in a maelstrom.

Atmospheric conditions for all of these events were different.

But mountains create their own weather, or at least they do on large planets like Ius Prime, and some meteorologists as well as astrogeologists claim that the same sort of phenomenon is going on here.

Whatever the cause, though, the idea of a ship heading to Madreperla to probe the Nájar Crater sounds like a date with disaster.

Yet W&D managed to get insurance for the voyage. The *Gabriella's* insurance paid out survivor benefits to each crewmember's family, something that an insurance company would not have done if they deemed the journey reckless.

Beta Linde claims that Ferguson and his crew had a new plan of attack for the crater. She believes they were going to approach fact-finding in a new way—or rather, she says, a new old-fashioned way.

"Giles believed it was tech that activated the maelstroms. No ship went into that area without scanning the area first. He thinks the scans activated something, and then the proximity of engines and other tech aggravated it, like some sort of defense," she told me late one afternoon at the bar.

No one else was there, although I wish there were. I wanted to check to see if this sounded strange to other ears.

I thought it sounded like justification, but I did end up contacting Imelda afterwards.

"He mentioned something like that to me," she told me, "but the research doesn't bear it out. The ships that approached the crater are all different, made of different materials, and using different frequencies in their scans. The tech isn't similar at all."

That's what I had found in the scientific treatises I'd located. I didn't say so, though, not willing to change the direction of the conversation.

"Still," she said, her tone musing, "something convinced the insurance companies that this particular trip was viable. Something made them think this trip did not have the same risk that a trip to Nájar Crater usually has."

I asked her if she believes that Ferguson found a way to beat the crater.

"Clearly he didn't," she said. "The entire lost ship tells us that. But did others think he had a way? Maybe. He convinced someone. Because insurance companies do their best to deny payouts, and they granted the payouts fast in this particular instance."

They did. That's one of the mysteries of the *Gabriella*. Survivors from other lost ships usually have to wait the five years required by law to receive any benefits at all.

While it took five years to declare the crew dead and thus release their estates, the insurance companies waived the right to wait, and sent survivors benefits immediately. They didn't even include the documents usually sent with an early release, saying that the money had to be returned should it turn out that the ship wasn't lost after all.

When I contacted the insurance companies about this unusual change in policy, no representative would talk to me about any claims besides my own, citing privacy concerns. I got several survivors to waive the privacy claims, but the companies still wouldn't talk to me, and the survivors eventually withdrew their support, afraid, they said, that they might lose their funding after all.

That money is important because it was, in many instances, the only money survivors received for their lost family members. Most lived on the edge, paying bills with each payout, never saving, and owning little more than the clothing on their backs.

The survivors usually had jobs, but the money that the crew member made was often the difference between living a financially solid existence, and living below the poverty line.

Many families had to leave Ochoa Star Port because they no longer had any connection to a ship. Even more families left Ciudad Orilla because it was much too expensive to live there on one salary.

And then there is the trauma of loss.

Belinda Pete told me she hasn't slept well since word of the ship's loss reached her. She doesn't want to believe that Corey is dead, but she needs to believe it to claim death benefits.

She waited the full five years before filing a single claim, including insurance, and she still feels guilty about it.

"If I fall into a sound sleep," she said, "I wake up within an hour, hearing his laugh. He says, *Why'd you lose faith, Belinda? You know I been in worse situations than this one.*"

6

BUT WE DON'T KNOW IF HE'S BEEN IN WORSE SITUATIONS, because we don't know exactly what happened to the *Gabriella*.

What we do know is this:

On the Tuesday after launch, Ferguson contacts Naomi Ruhl of the *Angelina*, asking if she'll be in the vicinity of Madreperla on Friday.

I'm thinking we need a few ships to back us up, he says. *We'll pay for the time you take away from your core mission. Not a lot, mind you, but enough for peace of mind.*

"If he had really needed extra ships, he would have asked me on Sunday," she says now. "I saw him. I even shared some of that skunky beer with him outside the Elizabeta. We talked about our upcoming trips, as best we could without giving away too many secrets, and he seemed confident, maybe overly so. But the man I talked to two days later wasn't confident at all. I asked him what changed, and he said nothing, really. It was just that he'd been thinking about other ships that had gone to Madreperla, and the ones that survived had sister ships in the vicinity."

The *Angelina* isn't a sister ship. She doesn't have the infinity build. She's not a former military vehicle. She's a long-haul cargo ship without a lot of maneuverability.

That Ferguson called her a sister ship seems odd. Perhaps he felt a kinship to her captain. Or perhaps he saw all private vessels as sister ships.

Nothing in the record clarifies that, and neither does anything in Ferguson's conversation with Naomi.

At the moment of the conversation, the *Angelina* has a choice of two routes, one that will take her closer to Madreperla. But Naomi worries that her definition of close is different from his.

She asks him to clarify what he wants.

You know the history of Nájar Crater, he says. *If we run into difficulty, I want to know that someone can reach us relatively quickly.*

She's never heard him sound this nervous before, nor has she ever heard him ask for help. The *Gabriella* has been in tight spots before. Once she limped back to Ochoa with half a working engine and, rumor has it, short most of the ammunition needed to run the weapons systems.

That crew wouldn't talk about what happened, although one crew member—not Ferguson—told Naomi that they had nearly died out there.

When Naomi asked Ferguson about it weeks later, he laughed that story off and said his people exaggerated.

That was always his response when it seemed that the *Gabriella* had gotten into situations that spiraled out of control.

We made it through, he said to anyone who asked. *We were fine. Sometimes people exaggerate.*

And sometimes people understate what they have gone through. Ferguson is known for understatement. Early in his career, he had his crew sign nondisclosure agreements before they could board not, they say, because he was handling confidential materials, but because he didn't like gossip or rumor surrounding any of his trips.

Over time, he dropped that requirement, but he still preferred crew members who tended toward silence. Even Corey Burfet, who loved a good story, never told one about his journeys on the *Gabriella*.

When asked—and Belinda asked a lot—Corey would say that of all the ships he served on the *Gabriella* was the calmest, the easiest, and the least prone to disaster.

But Naomi Ruhl believes that Ferguson was sensing disaster early in the journey to Nájar Crater.

"Not the kind of disaster that would make him turn around," she says. "But enough of one to make him more cautious than usual."

She is not the only captain he contacted that Tuesday.

Mercedes LaCoste of the *Selena* says she heard from him as well.

"He sounded almost angry," she said. "As if he didn't want to be talking to me. He demanded to know where the *Selena* was and what our heading was. I normally wouldn't have told him, but I'd already heard about the journey to Nájar Crater, so I knew we were on a different mission. I gave him our coordinates, and he cursed. When I asked him what was wrong, he said we were just too far away."

During that day of contacts, he also reaches Tomito Gerhardt, captain of the *Decker*. Gerhardt wouldn't talk to me for this project, but according to his testimony at the very first inquest into the loss of the *Gabriella*, he said this:

Giles promised me twice our usual daily fee if I brought the *Decker* to Madreperla. He wanted me to remain within an hour's range of the moon itself, but I wanted to see what he was doing. So I instructed our people to orbit Madreperla after the *Gabriella* went into the atmosphere.

It was a fateful decision for many reasons, one that resulted in Gerhardt losing his credentials. He now lives off his pension, which proved untouchable despite a series of lawsuits going after every bit of money he ever made.

The *Decker* is closer to Madreperla than the *Gabriella* is when Ferguson starts contacting other ships. In addition to Naomi Ruhl, Mercedes LaCoste, and Tomito Gerhardt, several other captains also receive requests from Ferguson. All of their ships are too far away.

Even if they weren't, some of those captains might not have gone to Madreperla, no matter how much Ferguson offered to pay.

"He doesn't speak to me for nearly five years, and suddenly he wants me to do him a favor?" Orion Newbawer, captain of the *Vista*, said. "I mean, I'm sorry he's dead, but I don't regret refusing him for one instant. Think about what happened to everyone who tried to help him. They've all been ruined. Maybe if he consulted with me before he left for Nájar Crater, I could've talked him out of it."

Then Orion laughed without humor. He shakes his head.

"I'm delusional," he said. "I couldn't talk Giles out of anything. No one could. Not when he had his mind set on something."

Some of the captains believe the journey to Nájar Crater was Ferguson's idea, not a directive from W&D. Records are unclear on this. Nothing indicates who decided that an exploration of Nájar Crater would be both possible and lucrative.

"Giles did a lot of shady things," Orion said. "Not many people will tell you that, because he's dead, and because…"

His voice trailed off, but he looked at me, as if he expects me to understand.

"It was always about the money for him," Orion said. "The money and being first. Being the one who actually conquered something everyone else believes is impossible. Sometimes we have to listen, you know? Sometimes we have to understand that everyone else has failed for a reason."

He shook a finger at me, his voice rising.

"Smart captains don't go near Nájar Crater, not after everything that's happened there. Everyone pretends that Giles was a smart captain, but he never was. The trip to Nájar Crater was a suicide mission. And the tragedy is that he took others down with him."

7

ACCORDING TO THE RECORD, COMPILED IN THE VARIOUS inquests after the loss of the *Gabriella*, she arrives on Madreperla in the early hours of the morning on a Wednesday, shortly after Ferguson contacted all those captains.

The *Gabriella* sends automated notifications to W&D, stating she is in orbit around Madreperla. There is no more information than that. W&D does not require any progress reports along the journey, just location reports.

There is nothing in the official record that tells us why Ferguson wanted another ship nearby. Nor are there records from the *Gabriella*. Her internal logs disappeared along with her. Ferguson never practiced off-ship backup protocols, even though they had become standard.

"He said he would have made off-ship backups had he been captain of a government ship," Imelda told me in our longest interview, the one that focused mostly on Ferguson. "But he was leery of reporting anything when he was on a commercial vessel. He figured too much information invited poachers and pirates. He didn't even like pinging locations, but he couldn't avoid that requirement."

There are no records of poachers or pirates in the area, at least not in the official information.

During a direct question session at the second inquest, the *Decker's* Gerhardt says he saw no evidence of pirating or poaching while he was observing the *Gabriella* from afar.

Gerhardt: No one in their right mind poaches ships near Nájar Crater. And there's very little to pirate. Generally speaking, pirates don't work that close to Ius Prime, anyway. The star port frightens them. They like remote areas, where they have no chance of getting caught.

Counsellor: So you do not believe the *Gabriella* was attacked by outside agents in orbit or on the ground.

Gerhardt: I know they were not attacked in orbit. We would have seen the readings. I have no idea what happened to them on the ground.

Counsellor: In other words, they could have been attacked.

Gerhardt: I don't speculate. I don't have the evidence.

Counsellor: Did you attack them?

Gerhardt: [angrily] Hell no! How could you even suggest that? We have logs, records—

Counsellor: Which could have been doctored.

Gerhardt: They're not doctored. I gave them to you people for certification.

Counsellor: Not to us.

Chief Judge: To the court. We have certified the *Decker's* logs, and found no evidence of tampering. Move along, counsellor. This line of questioning is wasting the review board's time.

Pirates sounds romantic and terrifying at the same time, as do poachers, but the chief judge of that inquest, and the judicial review boards of later inquests, continued to find the *Decker's* logs credible. Those logs show no record of outside activity from unidentified vessels.

Besides, if such vessels had existed and attacked from the ground, the maelstrom that ultimately enveloped the *Gabriella* would, logically, have taken them too.

But the *Decker* does not see all. There is a scanner dead zone on the far side of Madreperla, at least from the *Decker's* location. To get a full reading from the entire moon, the *Decker* would have had to orbit as well, and Gerhardt decides not to. He does not want to call attention to himself.

It seems that he was successful in that. There is no record of communication between the *Decker* and the *Gabriella* during the hours after the *Gabriella's* arrival.

As far as we can tell, the crew of the *Gabriella* believe they are alone. The frantic contacts to other captains have eased, and the *Gabriella* settles into her orbit. Once the trajectory gets established, the *Gabriella* pings W&D.

The notification system is primitive by design. Apparently Ferguson's paranoia is infectious. Even the location tracking is vague. Rather than sending detailed coordinates from the ship, the ship sends one set of coordinates and describes the maneuvers it has entered into.

According to the information in W&D's files, the *Gabriella* slips into orbit around Madreperla at 02:34 that Wednesday morning. (All times and dates from here on out will follow the Old Spacer system for consistency.) The orbit lasts twenty hours, which some experts in the various inquests considered too long, while others considered it too short.

If the slide into orbit around Madreperla goes the way it went for Orion Newbawer's ship, the *Vista* on her final visit, then the *Gabriella* is on full alert, with the entire crew active.

The first orbit usually establishes systems. Ferguson will be focused on the orbit itself and the challenges it poses to the *Gabriella*. His bridge crew monitors the readouts, makes slight adjustments, and keeps track of the pressure on the ship herself.

This is the first test of the *Gabriella* on this journey. As a space-to-land vehicle, she needs to make adjustments before she enters Madreperla's gravity.

In order to land, the *Gabriella* must deploy her landing gear, add even more protections to her large engines, and activate the land engines. She can do none of that as she enters the atmosphere.

This is one of the design flaws that led the military to retire the infinity design, at least as a space-to-land vehicle. Ferguson has dealt with this quirk of the *Gabriella* for his entire captaincy of the ship and is used to the problem.

If Ferguson follows his usual practices, he will not even suggest making the landing adjustments until he is certain the ship can land.

That means he must complete his scans and decide if he is going to complete the most dangerous part of this mission before he gives the order to send the ship into Madreperla's atmosphere.

On the second orbit around Madreperla, the crew probably watches the light change across the moon's surface. Madreperla, named for its luminescence when viewed from Ius Prime, is even brighter from orbit.

The dirt on the surface of the smaller land mass on Madreperla reflects light. The moon's inherent brightness causes problems for any ship attempting to scan.

The *Vista* had to adjust its screens so that the crew could see the surface all the way around the moon. Other ships alter their portals with a built-in shading so that the light off that dirt does not hurt the eye.

Even with the protections, the light traveling across the surface is beautiful. It illuminates certain geographical features, like the three greenish oceans, and leaves others in shadow, like the mountain peaks around Nájar Crater.

In the previous century, an orbit around Madreperla was considered one of the Sixteen Wonders of the sector, and was a specialty of View Tours run by some of the cruise ship lines. But once Ochoa issued its warnings about Nájar Crater, the orbit became costly and prohibitive. Each passenger had to sign off on the special permits, and few agreed to do that.

Still, crews that got to see the light travel across Madreperla felt lucky. Everyone who served on a ship that orbited Madreperla knew they were seeing one of the most unusual sites in the sector.

Every crew member I spoke to who traveled to Madreperla described that moment—usually on the second pass—where they crowded around the portals and ran to the view galleries to catch a glimpse.

Ferguson is not a sentimental man, nor one with much appreciation for natural beauty. He's probably ignoring his crew's enthusiasm, or raging against it. If he's watching the surface at all, he's trying to see what's around the mountain range and Nájar Crater itself.

If he remains true to past practice, he's also running scans of every inch of the surface, as well as more than a dozen scans of Nájar Crater. He will then huddle with his senior researcher, as well as his science and engineering staff to see if his scans line up with the scans the *Gabriella* got before the ship left Ius Prime.

That will take hours, which is probably why the *Gabriella's* status in orbit is so long.

"I think they found problems," Imelda said. "I think there were just enough inconsistencies to make Giles worry. Because normally, he would have taken an hour or two to review everything before heading to the surface."

But there are a lot of problems with that surface that Ferguson and the *Gabriella* have never encountered before. There's no good landing area near Nájar Crater. The mountains are too steep, and the ice shelves around the crater are very unstable.

"They probably had a place to land mapped out ahead of time," Orion said. "I would guess it was on the northwest side of the crater, where the foothills form a kind of flat land."

But it is possible that a closer scan of that landing area proves unsatisfactory. The *Gabriella* is like no other ship that has tried to land near Nájar Crater, at least according to the records kept by the star port.

The *Gabriella* is larger in general, and that infinity shape makes her longer than most ships. The landing gear is on one of the outside edges of the shape. Meaning if you were to look at the ship from the ground, you would see the entire infinity shape facing you, rather than the edges of it, lying flat. The placement of the landing gear protects the bubbles around the engines, by keeping them high off the ground. It also allows the landing gear to be short, instead of long enough to accommodate the width of those bubbles.

If you only look at where the landing gear touches the ground, then the footprint of the *Gabriella* is small. But if you take into account the width, with the bubbles around the edges, the *Gabriella* is quite large.

If the *Gabriella* lands too close to the foothills, they will brush up against the engine bubbles. If the *Gabriella* moves closer to Nájar Crater, then she risks putting too much weight on a shelf rather than a solid piece of land.

Ice shelves surround the rest of Nájar Crater. The ice shelves are wider, but much more dangerous, given what happened to the *Maria Segunda* and the ships that followed.

It is possible for the *Gabriella* to land in front of those foothills, if the scanned and recorded measurements are correct. But it is distinctly possible that there has been erosion or that there are boulders or other debris that make landing the *Gabriella* difficult at best.

She has hovering capability, and perhaps Ferguson decided as he got closer to Madreperla to hover, instead of land.

That decision might explain why he contacted other captains, asking them to back him up, if possible.

There is some evidence that the backwash from a traditional hover is one of the things that triggers a maelstrom. Hovering near Nájar Crater is not recommended.

Still, some of the spacers I spoke to believe it's possible Ferguson made this very decision. The *Gabriella's* engines are different than all of the others that came before her. They vibrate at a different frequency.

The *Gabriella* is the first (former) military vehicle that will get this close to Nájar Crater, that we know of, anyway. And a lot of experts believe that the differences in the engines will make it safer for the *Gabriella* to attempt a hover rather than a landing.

"I wouldn't do it," Orion told me, "but then I wouldn't do half the stuff that Giles did and got away with. Still, just because the engines are different doesn't guarantee that the ship is safer. There's a distinct possibility that the differences might have triggered a worse maelstrom, like the one from the…whatsis? Maria whatever?"

"*Maria Segunda,*" I said softly, not wanting to interrupt an interview subject but wanting him to move forward.

"Yeah, that one. How come that ship experienced a worse maelstrom than any other? Was it the engines? Has anyone checked?"

I did not know the answer, and said so.

"Exactly," Orion said. "There are too many risks associated with Nájar Crater. I might specialize in risk, but there's a difference between doing something risky with the possibility of a great payoff, and doing something risky that will have no good payoff at all."

Either Ferguson's calculations of risk are different from Orion's or Ferguson knows of mitigating factors that Orion isn't aware of.

Because, after twenty hours, the *Gabriella* breaks orbit and heads to the surface of Madreperla.

Images the *Decker* took of the *Gabriella* before her descent into the atmosphere show that she has deployed her landing gear. However, the *Gabriella* can hover with the gear activated.

The hover command activates the same engines that the *Gabriella* uses to land. These engines are smaller, and placed at six points around the infinity shape. They are useless in space, although some military captains have used them as thrusters to change direction in the middle of a battle.

These six small engines take over the propulsion of the ship once she enters Madreperla's atmosphere. The large main engines shut down—again, something best done in space—and for half an orbit, the *Gabriella* will float while the smaller engines prepare for their part of the mission.

Eventually, when the captain or the chief engineer decides the moment is right, the smaller engines will thrust the *Gabriella* out of orbit and into the atmosphere.

The ship literally dives out of orbit. Once she leaves space, her rotations cease. The smaller part of the infinity shape leads, with the larger part following. The main bridge is located where the two shapes cross, a protected point in space, but almost a bullseye once the ship tips up on its end on land.

All of that factors into where the *Gabriella* will stop, but most likely, none of it goes through Ferguson's consciousness as he gives the orders to dive into the atmosphere. By then the landing location is chosen, and every contingency has already been planned for.

Or so one would hope.

8

A DIVE INTO THE ATMOSPHERE ON AN INFINITY-SHAPED ship feels different than a usual trip through atmosphere. The ride is often bumpy in the thicker atmosphere of a planet like Ius Prime.

But Madreperla's atmosphere is relatively thin. Even in a badly designed ship, the trip would seem easier than a trip into Ius Prime.

"In most ships," said Lieutenant Commander Wiley Crawford, who spent years aboard the *Gabriella* before she was decommissioned, "the trip through atmosphere is theoretical, unless you're watching it from one of the view decks."

On the view decks, the pristine vision from orbit turns into a haze of light and fire. If the ship is diving fast enough, that light appears as lines of brightness before it completely engulfs the ship. Once the ship actually enters the atmosphere, then the light changes again, becoming less intense.

If you're on the bridge, or monitoring the systems, you will see none of that. Instead, the heat shields will deploy. External temperature readings will rise, and the ship—any ship—will compensate.

An infinity ship, like the *Gabriella,* will float for a few minutes as the main engines shut down and the landing engines deploy. When Lieutenant Commander Wiley served on the *Gabriella*, the bridge was quiet most of the time, so he noticed the background hum. It would change with the change of the engines.

The hum would stop—at which point he realized he had even been hearing it, because it had become one of those noises his brain routinely ignored. The silence would seem almost palpable. Then, a few seconds later, the smaller engines would activate. They didn't hum; they had a high-pitched whine Wiley found annoying. That whine grew more intense as the ship plunged into atmosphere or used the engines as thrusters.

It's impossible to know how the crew of Ferguson's *Gabriella* experiences entry into the atmosphere. Some, those without duties during landing, probably do crowd into the view decks, which line the edges of the ovals on the infinity design.

Most of the crew, however, are probably working. They will make a mental note of the shift in the noise inside the bridge, or the loss of the natural shudder that the larger engines make. They might notice the float. And they will know, from their equipment if nothing else, when the smaller engines activate.

Because Madreperla's atmosphere is thin, the trip through it is relatively short, and probably not as dramatic as entering thicker atmosphere, like that around Ius Prime.

And the *Decker* reported that the *Gabriella's* descent seemed both rapid and abrupt. One moment it was orbiting Madreperla, and the next it was plunging toward Nájar Crater.

The readings received by W&D confirm that. Trips through atmosphere are usually rapid to prevent strain on whatever engine is being used. The trip that the *Gabriella* took was faster than recommended in those conditions.

"Giles hated transitions," Imelda told me. "He always had my team research the best way from one place to another. When that concerned entering atmosphere, he wanted it over quickly. I always had the sense it made him nervous."

The trip toward Nájar Crater should make him nervous. It's the most dangerous trip he ever takes, at least according to the records remaining of his career.

He has to have known that. He has to have prepared for it.

Because he is not the kind of man who ignores the difficulties he faces.

He embraces them instead.

9

THE DIFFICULTIES ARE PRESENT FROM THE MOMENT Ferguson plunges the *Gabriella* between those mountain ranges. The ship speeds downward in a controlled fall. One final automated message sent to W&D placed the *Gabriella* 150 miles off the surface of Madreperla. If we map her speed and trajectory, we see that she probably landed fifteen minutes after that last ping.

If she landed. If she didn't crash. If she didn't encounter problems.

From here forward, the record is thin. We know that the *Gabriella* is plunging downward. We assume, because we have those last contacts, that all is working perfectly.

But because no parts of the *Gabriella* have ever been found, we do not know exactly what happened to her.

Here are the scenarios based on the hypotheses put forth in all the official inquests and insurance investigations.

Scenario One: Catastrophic Systems Failure. Inadequately maintained ships like the *Gabriella* can suffer systems failure, usually at the moment of greatest stress. In the cool language of the first inquest:

> The *Gabriella* did not follow maintenance protocols for a ship of her age and designation. What protocols she did follow were often designed to augment existing systems not to repair them. Some of the systems with which she was outfitted did not work well with other systems already existing on the ship. There is no record of further maintenance that would enable those systems to work together…

> With the stress of a difficult entry into Madreperla's atmosphere, and with the force of even a minor maelstrom, the *Gabriella* might have suffered a complete systems collapse as she reached her destination. By all accounts, however, the maelstrom the *Gabriella* encountered was *not* minor.

The dry language does not convey what happens at moments like that. But the mission I set for myself in writing this piece is to reconstruct the final days of the *Gabriella* to the best of my ability.

So I researched ships that had suffered catastrophic systems failure as they enter the atmosphere of Madreperla. I found a handful of ships over the century that fit that description, but all of the ships crashed with no survivors.

The remaining record from those ships is technical. Data sent from a dying ship back to the home port, the rest of a fleet, or the company that owns the ship. The technical record, filled with error messages, and speculation, tells a tale of crews that try one thing after another, seeing if those things will work.

But the technical record does not reveal when the crew knows it is doomed. Or if the crew ever makes that realization. Do they work until the end?

I do not know.

What I do find is a single record of a woman who survived the crash of a vessel on Perlagris, one of Ius Prime's other moons. It is the only record I could find that even partially answered my questions—and it only did so because Perlagris has a similar gravity and atmosphere to its sister moon, Madreperla.

The woman, Estelle Lundgren, owned *Sam's Bark,* a much smaller vessel than the *Gabriella*. *Sam's Bark* was a standard military decommissioned space-to-land vehicle. It held only sixteen passengers. The configuration was rectangular. The ship had no separation between its bridge, which is called a cockpit on the specs, and the passenger seating.

Lundgren was traveling with what she called a "resource" team to see land she was purchasing in the shadow of the only mountains on Perlagris. There is no crater in that area, and very little vegetation. Traveling to and landing on Perlagris is not restricted by Star Port Ochoa or any other entity.

Sam's Bark—named as a joke by a previous owner—was not in the best of shape, but Lundgren and her board of directors figured it could make a simple trip from their main vessel, the *Samantha*, to Perlagris.

They were wrong.

Lundgren survived the crash, and testified at the inquest on Ochoa. In her opening statement, she made it clear that she was not piloting the vessel. She had no piloting skills whatsoever. She said, "I hire people for things like that."

After some disparaging remarks about *Sam's Bark* and the recommendations from the *Samantha* crew, Lundgren's opening statement described what happened before the crash.

We were strapped into our chairs for the promised twenty-minute flight. We were comfortable, although the interior had the faint scent of burning rubber, which I mentioned to Lucien Makadi, our pilot.

He said that the system had been down earlier, but the engineers checked it over, and we had nothing to worry about. So we settled into our seats, and watched as we traveled into the atmosphere, something that always made me a bit uncomfortable.

I was sitting next to the exterior wall, which actually grew warm. I was about to ask if that was normal when warning bells started blaring from the cockpit.

I asked what was wrong, but no one answered me. The crew was shouting at each other, lights from even more warnings flashing red and yellow across their faces.

Put on your suits! Put on your suits! Makadi yelled at us, while someone else asked if we should get out of our seats or stay strapped in.

Yes, get out! he yelled. *We have two escape pods. Yours is in the back of the ship. We will follow.*

The three of us passengers grabbed our environmental suits, and I made the decision to get us onto the pod before we put the suits on. I think that saved our lives.

The interior was really hot, and I was sweating so badly that the environmental suit someone handed me almost slipped through my fingers. I clutched the suit against my chest, and shoved my way to the pod.

Getting the pod door open was almost impossible. I didn't know the code, and when I yelled that, my voice didn't carry over the shouting in the cockpit. They were arguing about what to do next.

Enoch [her assistant] pushed me aside and slammed his palm against the controls. They lit up, but the door still didn't open. I pushed him back and entered the same code we had used to enter *Sam's Bark*.

That worked, and we tumbled inside, clutching our suits. Enoch hit the separation/escape button, which was all the control we had. There was no way to navigate that pod. It was designed to be used in space, not in atmosphere.

The pod jettisoned.

We tumbled, untethered, against each other, as the pod rolled its way down to the ground. I hit my chin, bit my tongue, lost my grip on the environmental suit, and tried to brace myself on the walls.

Thank the designers that the walls were soft, because if they were hard, we would have broken every bone in our bodies. As it was, someone's shoe slammed into my head, an arm whacked me in the stomach so hard that it knocked the air out of me, and the back of my hand hit someone in the face.

I couldn't tell whose body was hitting mine or how to get out of the way. I was dizzy from spinning and unable to breathe because I got hit so hard and then—blam!—it all stopped.

The impact knocked me back—I thought I had broken my neck at first—and it knocked the other two out. I couldn't get them off me, and I could barely move. I was pretty convinced we were all going to die there, but someone in that cockpit managed to send out a distress signal, which was the other thing that saved our lives.

Lundgren got away with broken ribs, one broken leg, a shattered cheekbone, and all kinds of soft tissue injuries.

Sam's Bark also crashed with its crew still inside. It looked like they made no effort to get to the second pod. They were still trying to right the ship when it crashed.

There are no recordings of what the crew said or what their plans were, whether they knew they were about to die or if they thought they still had time to solve the system's failure and make it all work.

From the moment *Sam's Bark* entered the atmosphere to the moment of the crash took five minutes and 43 seconds. There is no record of how long the pod tumbled and fell. It landed two miles away from *Sam's Bark*, which was probably a blessing, since *Sam's Bark* left a scar on the land for another half mile. *Sam's Bark* threw off bits and pieces of itself, damaging everything in its wake.

The pod hit the ground directly, digging itself into a small hole. Rescuers only found Lundgren because the pod also carried a distress beacon that both flared and sent out some kind of pulse.

Clearly *Sam's Bark* is a much smaller ship than the *Gabriella*. There is no evidence that anyone launched escape pods as the *Gabriella* ran into trouble. Nor is there evidence—from orbit, anyway—that the *Gabriella* crash landed. Or if she had crash landed, that she was intact when she did so.

Nájar Crater is so large, however, that the *Gabriella* could have spiraled out of control and landed inside the crater, and it would be impossible to see what happened from space.

Scans of the surface from orbit do not show the remains of any crashed ship that match the *Gabriella's* specs. Nor do later scans, exploring two land masses on Madreperla, show anything that might be linked to the *Gabriella*.

She might have landed in one of Madreperla's oceans, but she would have had to have broken up upon impact, because scans run on Madreperla would have found something as large as the *Gabriella* even if she had crashed into one of the oceans.

The other possibility is that the *Gabriella* suffered a systems failure so extreme that she exploded as she traveled through the heat shield or before she landed.

The explosion itself would have had to have been catastrophic, breaking the ship in small pieces because, again, scans were never able to find large pieces of anything resembling the *Gabriella*.

The question is, though, what would have happened inside the *Gabriella* as the tension unfolded.

By all accounts, Ferguson ran a tight ship. The crew did not scream at each other as the crisis unfolded. There were no passengers to off-load, and the crew members below decks might not have even known that a catastrophic systems failure was occurring.

So the attitude inside the ship probably depended on where crew members were located in the ship: those who were at their posts, be it on the bridge or in engineering or even in the cargo bays, probably had an idea that the *Gabriella* was in trouble. Those sleeping in their cabins after their shifts or sitting in the view decks probably had no idea that they were about to die.

"When I served with Giles," Imelda said, "we were in more than one tough spot. A couple of times it looked like the ship was going to sustain serious damage or wasn't going to make it out of the situation. Giles and the bridge crew continued working as if nothing was wrong. They might have worked faster, but they didn't get upset. They had a shorthand, a way of discussing things that I couldn't entirely access, because I wasn't regular crew. But I always felt confident that if anyone could solve the problem at hand, Giles Ferguson could."

Scenario Two: The Land/Ice Shelf the *Gabriella* Landed on Was Unable to Hold Her Weight.

While it sounds similar to what happened to the *Maria Segunda*, it is not. The *Maria Segunda* spent a relatively quiet night on an ice shelf over the crater before the maelstrom hit her. She was able to launch herself back into orbit, destroying the ice shelf in the process.

The maelstrom damaged the ship; the ship was not damaged before the maelstrom hit.

The *Maria Segunda* decided to land on an ice shelf instead of on the land rim. There were rims available, but farther away.

The crater's rims are a combination of thick, solid edges made of the same bedrock as the mountains alongside the crater, and ice shelves that jet out in certain parts of the crater's northern side.

If the *Gabriella* landed on an ice shelf, and it collapsed, the collapse had to be swift enough to prevent the *Gabriella* from engaging her landing engines and launching herself into orbit, the way that the *Maria Segunda* had done.

There is scant evidence that the *Gabriella* landed intact. But there is evidence that at least two of the ice shelves around Nájar Crater became smaller after the *Gabriella's* arrival. Scans of the surface show that the ice shelves have a completely different shape than they did when the *Gabriella* scanned her.

But those later scans were completed months after the *Gabriella* disappeared, and there is no evidence as to when the shelves changed shape. Nor is there evidence that the *Gabriella* landed on any of those shelves.

The various landing sites that the *Gabriella* had chosen were nowhere near those ice shelves.

However, as experts in the inquests reminded the courts, a ship in distress does not follow its original plan. Nor does a ship landing somewhere dangerous. Should a closeup scan show a problem impossible to see from orbit, the ship would have chosen another landing site.

There is no way to know if the *Gabriella* did this, if her landing site was unstable, and if she was unable to hover or move away from that site in time.

This seems to be the least likely of the scenarios about what happened to the *Gabriella*.

But we cannot rule it out entirely.

Scenario Three: The *Gabriella* Was Completely Demolished by a Maelstrom.

This is the most likely scenario and the one that two of the six inquests ruled as the cause of the *Gabriella's* disappearance. The *Decker's* logs of a scan of Madreperla taken shortly after the *Gabriella* plunged into its atmosphere show that a maelstrom has already started.

Gerhardt of the *Decker* expects to get some kind of signal from Ferguson, but nothing happens. Gerhardt does not move the *Decker* from its position outside of orbit, nor does he step up scans, despite the recommendations from various members of his crew.

He keeps to the usual scans, one every thirty minutes.

The second scan shows that the maelstrom has grown to monster proportions and, like the maelstrom that chased the *Maria Segunda* off Madreperla, this maelstrom is extending its reach a hundred miles above Madreperla's surface.

This maelstrom is half the width of Nájar Crater and is exceptionally long. It is also the most violent maelstrom on record, with winds clocking in at 300 miles per hour, filled with debris and rock and materials that do not register as anything but heavy solids in the *Decker's* scans.

Still, the *Decker* does not move closer.

"I was waiting for a distress signal," Gerhardt told each inquest, his answer exactly the same whenever anyone asked him why the *Decker* never moved.

In the first inquest, some members of his crew speculated that he did not want to get close to Madreperla for fear of harming the *Decker*. But in the second, bridge crew stipulated under oath that he stated he *wanted* the *Gabriella* to be destroyed so that he could take over the various jobs that Ferguson and the *Gabriella* stole from him.

The *Decker* didn't qualify for most of those jobs because of its size and capabilities. A later investigation, paid for by Gerhardt, states there is no proof of those statements or of any jealousy between Gerhardt and Ferguson, or between the *Decker* and the *Gabriella*.

Actions that look sinister in one light have a perfectly rational explanation when viewed from another perspective. The key perspective on Captain Gerhardt's behavior is this: He voluntarily went to Madreperla to assist Captain Ferguson the moment Captain Ferguson asked. Other ship's captains, who received the same request, turned it down outright or showed up too late to do anything except run scans of Madreperla.

Unlike Captain Ferguson, Captain Gerhardt has seen the damage caused by a mild maelstrom firsthand. Captain Gerhardt knew the dangers of that section of Madreperla. Knowing those dangers made him willing to help, while making him cautious about the best way to do so.

Decker's experience with a maelstrom-damaged ship happened during a brief military career. He worked search-and-rescue between Ius Prime and its moons for a year.

During that time, a ship named the *Hestia* got caught in what records describe as a "mild maelstrom" near

Nájar Crater's surface. The *Hestia* was a small ship, like *Sam's Bark*. The *Hestia's* pilot, remembering what she had heard about the possible causes of a maelstrom, sent one gigantic blast from her engines to launch her out of Madreperla's atmosphere, and then shut the engines down entirely.

Whether that caused the maelstrom to recede or whether it had been small to begin with isn't known. What is known is that by the time the *Hestia* reached orbit, she couldn't activate her engines and all of her systems were down.

Her tiny crew had worn their environmental suits throughout the entire mission, so the crew was in good physical shape. They were able to survive the five-hour wait it took for the nearest vessel, the *Rauaran*—which happened to be military—to respond to their distress signals.

Gerhardt served belowdecks on the *Rauaran*. He was not part of the actual rescue, but he helped load what remained of the *Hestia* in the cargo bay.

The *Rauaran's* crew used a grappler to bring the *Hestia* inside the bay. The grappler didn't hold the ship in place: instead, the grappler's claws broke holes in the *Hestia's* exterior. When the *Rauaran's* crew noticed that, they tried to unhook the grappler, which threatened to destroy what remained of the *Hestia* entirely.

So they dragged her inside, doing their best not to make the holes created by the claws any larger.

Once the doors closed on the cargo bay, Gerhardt and his crew extracted the claws by hand. They did so because the *Hestia*'s exterior had become as thin as paper.

The ship's surface wasn't scarred or damaged in the obvious and expected sense of something that had encountered a large wind. There were no dents or holes from contact with objects swirling inside the maelstrom.

Instead, the ship's exterior had been worn away, peeled back layer by layer, in the way that nail file would rub away callused skin.

The ship was no longer a ship, not really. It was a husk, fragments that—had the *Rauaran* not arrived quickly—would have slowly come apart and separated into space.

At the second inquest, Gerhardt testified, "I think the *Gabriella* was scrubbed away to nothing, exposing its interior and its crew to the elements. I was afraid if we got too close, we would get sucked into that powerful vortex as well."

"Even though you were in space?" the counsellor asked.

"There are reports of ships being sucked into the atmosphere by one of these maelstroms," Gerhardt had replied, and the Counsellor had left it at that.

Which is too bad, because Gerhardt is only partially correct. There are *unverified* reports of ships being pulled out of orbit on Madreperla, near Nájar Crater, by something resembling a maelstrom.

But a weather event cannot operate outside of atmosphere, and there is no evidence of any mechanical source for the maelstrom itself.

That inquest was tasked with two jobs: figuring out whether the *Gabriella* could be considered destroyed, and determining Gerhardt's role in her loss. That inquest ruled that the *Gabriella* was lost (this verdict would be questioned later), and that Gerhardt should lose his credentials and his personnel record would note that he showed "reckless disregard for the wellbeing of others," even though his own counsel argued that he had protected his crew.

Because Gerhardt believed the rumors that the maelstroms could reach into space, he was not charged with any crimes, such as failing to help another ship in distress. The loss of the credentials was considered enough.

In truth, it is more than enough. A spacer cannot travel on a commercial vehicle without credentials, and a spacer who is uninsured won't get work on the lowliest of vessels, even those that didn't care as much for official credentials as they did for experience.

The later investigation, cited above, was launched in part by Gerhardt to get his credentials—and his reputation—back. While he did receive partial reaccreditation, his reputation never recovered.

His decision to remain far away from Madreperla during the *Gabriella's* last few hours will have an impact on him and his career for the rest of his life.

But what of the *Gabriella?* Assuming she made it through the atmosphere unscathed, and landed safely, she still would have been engulfed by the maelstrom.

Records from more than a century of encounters with the maelstrom show that maelstroms strip layers from the ships in an instant. The ships that survive the maelstroms have a few things in common:

1. Those ships could launch out of the atmosphere with little more than a command. There were no systems that needed to be altered, no elaborate checklists that needed to be finished.

If the captain gave the order to launch, even from a hovering position, the ship could execute that order in less than a minute.

2. The ships have incredible, working, shields. The shields are not of the alternating kind, the kind designed to work against laser weapons and torpedoes. These ships have strong heat shields. These ships also have shields built for troubles encountered in atmosphere, shields that will remain in place in all kinds of weather, from ice storms to hurricane-force winds.

3. The maelstroms those ships encountered were relatively small. Maelstroms, like all storms, come in all sizes. The smaller maelstroms rarely grow taller than a mile, so the ship can outrun the maelstrom before the maelstrom completely destroys it.

The *Gabriella* has none of those advantages. Her weapons are useless against a storm like this. Her shields, which are old and designed for military encounters in deep space, work well enough in atmosphere but aren't designed to protect the ship in severe weather—whatever that weather might be.

And that's if her shields are at full capacity, which they are not. They are on an upgrades wish list submitted to W&D before the *Gabriella* left Ochoa. The plan was to complete the upgrades piecemeal, as the *Gabriella* went back and forth between Madreperla and Ochoa, reaping the rewards of her labors.

Even if the *Gabriella's* shields were top-of-the-line, they would not have aided her long. Her infinity shape does not allow her to shut down unusable parts of the vessel, moving ever inward to the more protected parts of the ship. There are no truly protected parts, not from something like this.

The *Gabriella* is designed to face threats in space, not threats on land, even though she has landing capabilities.

The biggest problem she has, though, when she is faced with a Nájar Crater maelstrom, is that the *Gabriella* does not have easy maneuverability. She is a large ship, and even though her landing engines double as launch engines, they do not have a lot of power. Unlike, say, the *Maria Segunda*, which had the engine strength to pull out of the severe wind-gravitational force of the maelstrom, the *Gabriella* does not.

The *Gabriella's* main engines are not designed to work with the landing engines. The *Gabriella* must use one system or the other, but she cannot use both at the same time.

Even the detachable bridge is not an option. It will take time to get the bridge crew to the other bridge, traversing half the length of the ship. Even if the bridge crew make it in record time, the engines on the detachable bridge are even weaker than the landing engines. There isn't enough power to propel any part of the *Gabriella* back into space, not when she is fighting something so massive on the ground.

How massive is this maelstrom?

Various scientific agencies have tried to answer that question. Based on the size of the maelstrom when it reached the edge of Madreperla's atmosphere, the measurements and scans the *Decker* took from her position in space, and the recordings taken from automated systems from Ochoa space port to buoys put into place all over that sector of space by the military, the consensus is that this maelstrom is the largest ever recorded on Madreperla.

It's not just the size of the maelstrom in width, depth, and height. It's also the wind. The wind speeds are terrifying, able to scour the surfaces of any spaceship even if the wind is not filled with debris.

But the winds are filled with debris—or something. As mentioned above, the *Decker's* scans read the wind as a solid, not as moving air. There is so much material in that moving air that it is like getting hit by a brick wall.

Later analysis, incomplete because none of the scans or readings were taken from inside Madreperla's atmosphere, show that the debris is made up of ice and rock pellets, bits of metal (perhaps from other ships), dust (probably from pulverized rock), and water.

It is impossible to know which of those things is more deadly to the *Gabriella*. Normally, the scientists say, water is the most destructive, particularly to ships like the *Gabriella*.

But this maelstrom's debris field is a stew of toxic materials.

"It's as if she hit a wall filled with sharp rotating blades," said scientist Baird Hampton who specializes in strange weather events. "Once she was in, there was no getting out."

"Think of one of those scraper things you use on orange peels," said scientist Ryan Northrup who has studied the maelstrom in the historical record, "only imagine it automated and out of control. *That's* what the *Gabriella* faced."

"High winds are dangerous," said scientist Aniyah Jesper, whose work focuses on hurricanes, typhoons, and other big weather events. "High wind scours whatever it touches, but high wind also breaks it apart. Water, on the other hand, binds the wind and the debris together, almost like a glue. Once the wind, water, and debris hit, at those speeds, no ship can get out, no matter how well designed."

No ship. So there was nothing the *Gabriella* could do, nothing any ship could have that would enable it to escape what the *Gabriella* faced.

No matter how hard Ferguson tried or how creative his crew got, they were never going to escape that maelstrom.

The question is when did they realize it? *Did* they realize it? Did they ever give up, or did they even have time to contemplate giving up?

There are no answers, of course. There's no record. There's only what happened before, in lesser maelstroms, the ones that people and ships survived.

10

"THE BRIDGE WAS MOSTLY EMPTY WHEN IT STARTED," said Zara Paldar, one of the survivors of the *Maria Segunda*, during her debrief. "Captain Nájar showed up just a few minutes before and was reviewing something on her board. I have no idea why she was there, because the entire crew was supposed to be asleep."

But it seems, at least according to Paldar, no one slept well that night. Something made them all uneasy, or so it seemed in hindsight. Or maybe, as one scholar suggested later, they were all so excited to be on Madreperla near the mysterious crater, that they simply couldn't close their eyes.

Paldar's debrief goes on for a long time, describing details of the ship and who stood where and what happened when. But the pertinent information to this project comes almost an hour in as she describes the maelstrom.

It rattled the ground, like an earthquake almost. And the captain was aware that we were on an ice shelf, so she was afraid we would tumble into the crater. She gave the order to hover the ship before the ice shelf collapsed, but the force of the engine exhaust melted part of the ice shelf. It fell apart, with large chunks of it falling into the water in the crater, splashing against the sides, and surprising us.

We thought the blackness we had seen was the darkness of a deep hole, not the edges of water. We thought the water started several meters below the rim of that crater.

We were surprised by that. We were surprised by a lot of things.

The maelstrom started from one of those splashes. A dagger of ice plunged into that water, and then an eddy started and it grew bigger and bigger, rising out of the crater.

By then, the captain had given the order to return to orbit, but the maelstrom engulfed us.

We're not supposed to hear anything small that hits the ship, but we could hear this, banging and clattering and slamming against us as if trying to get in.

Then there was the high-pitched hum, the strain on the engines, the tension in the body of the ship itself.

It felt like the ship would vibrate apart, and I thought for a while—what seemed like a while—that it would.

We were yanking our way out, like you would if your foot was caught in a vise. We were trying to pull ourselves upward, but that vise was tugging downward.

There was yelling—we had to yell, because the pounding and the hum and the vibration made it almost impossible to hear—but at the same time everyone seemed really calm.

That was Captain Nájar. She and First Officer Chandy, they acted like they had done this a thousand times before. They barked orders, and we followed them, and it kept us focused.

When the ship separated from the maelstrom, we zoomed upward and out so fast that the captain was worried we wouldn't be ready to launch into orbit. But we did, somehow, even though the ship was damaged. Even though the ship probably shouldn't have survived it.

That separation—it wasn't easy and it wasn't smooth. It was almost like the maelstrom let go. One moment we were being pulled downward, and the next, we were propelled forward, the way you are when someone is holding you back and they let go, but you're not ready for that release, and you stagger forward much too fast.

It felt like a contest of wills. We wanted out more than it wanted us.

That's how it seemed to me. Like we fought a live thing. And won.

Zara Paldar was not the only one who makes that analogy. Marina Vasilu, an engineer who was the only survivor of the *Illiana*, which broke apart in orbit after its encounter with the maelstrom, told the rescuers who pulled her from the escape pod:

> *Get us out of here! It's trying to kill us! It wants to destroy us!*

She said nothing else about her experience, and refused to talk about it ever again.

The handful of survivors all described noise and pounding and the incredible force of the maelstrom.

The *Gabriella* probably experiences the noise and pounding as well. The extreme pull of the maelstrom most likely tugs at the ship from all directions. The water and debris scour the exterior, first tearing the shields and then gouging into the ship herself.

If Ferguson remains true to form, he is calm on the bridge. He is probably yelling instructions at his crew due to the noise, although the interior noise might not be as loud on the *Gabriella*. The main engines are already shut down, and the smaller engines do not make the same kind of sounds.

The infinity shape probably twists and bends, maybe even tears apart. The *Gabriella* will seal any severed sections, but if the ship's exterior has too many holes, the ship will not be able to respond quickly enough to stop a full environmental failure.

Has Ferguson required his crew to suit up before they entered the atmosphere? He hasn't done that in the past, so most likely not. By the time there is the first sign of trouble, the chances for suiting up are probably gone.

Maybe some of the crew—those who are off-duty—run for the escape pods, but everyone who ever served with Ferguson doubts that.

"Giles liked people who faced problems head on, not people who ran from them," Imelda told me, and she was not the only one.

"The one thing I can guarantee," said Richard Hessecord, who served with Ferguson on other vessels, "is that everyone was working their tails off to the very end."

The *Gabriella* has enough crew members that each could patch a certain area, while others pour more power to the engines, maybe even try to run the small engines and the large one at the same time. Someone is probably boosting the shields.

But the *Gabriella* is being spun around inside the gigantic storm, being buffeted by extreme winds her shields are not built for, and being pummeled by water, debris, and metal fragments.

Most likely, say the experts (and the judges at three of the inquests), the ship breaks apart before her exterior scours off. But there is no way to know this. Maybe the exterior of the ship simply vanishes, leaving the bridge crew—maybe the entire crew—open to the elements.

In those conditions, the human body will last for perhaps fifteen seconds. Fifteen seconds sounds like a short time, but it is hellishly long as water whips your face, ice and rock sting your skin, and wind pulls your limbs apart. You cannot breathe, not just because of the water, but the wind makes breathing impossible as well.

You are not falling but you are not floating either. The wind holds you in whatever position it wants you in, until it disassembles you bit by bit.

No one has ever lived through this. No one has come back to report.

We can only assume, based on knowledge of human anatomy, knowledge of the ways wind strikes the body, knowledge of water spouts and wind-born debris, that—unless you fall unconscious as you tumble out of what remains of the ship—your last fifteen seconds are the most painful and terrifying of your entire life.

This is not an easy death. There is no easing into unconsciousness. Your lungs fill, your chest hurts, your eyes bulge, you swallow everything coming at you, and you cannot draw breath.

You are alone in this maelstrom. Even if your ship-mates tumble out of the ship beside you, you cannot see them or hear their cries. You might not be able to hear your own cries. You might not even know you're yelling. Or you might not be yelling at all, in this last desperate struggle to survive.

Do you wish for death or are you clawing at what surrounds you, trying to find purchase, maybe thinking you can get back into the ship, that someone will find you and pull you to safety?

All that is clear—not to you, but to us, and to all those inquests—is in a situation like that, as extreme as that maelstrom was, no ship will survive. No human will survive.

Humans will be broken into bits as small as the bits of dirt that spin inside this maelstrom, and even if those bits are carried away from Nájar Crater and fall on the ground, they will be impossible to recover.

The *Gabriella* is forever lost, as her crew is forever lost, as her story is forever lost.

What happened to her, and we can only guess, belongs to her alone. No matter how hard we search, we cannot find answers. Only more questions.

11

BECAUSE THERE ARE NO BODIES AND NO DEBRIS, BECAUSE the ship has completely vanished, many family members refused to accept that the ship was lost. The inquests were opened at the request of other family members, in different venues, trying to recover what was left of estates or to assign blame.

There is no blame to be had, except perhaps the greed that goes with this kind of exploration.

Some spacers believe there is no such thing as a maelstrom. They believe that what happens in Nájar Crater isn't a triggered storm but a weapon designed to keep people off the mineral-rich moon.

Perhaps the creators of that weapon are long gone, and the weapon still reacts to threats, even though it guards no one.

There is evidence to support that theory. The minerals and riches that exist in the crater don't appear elsewhere on Madreperla. The metals that are part of the debris field are tiny perfectly shaped balls, something many claim does not happen in nature.

Those balls are also made of a metal that we cannot identify.

But scientists point to natural substances that get made under stress, some of them once considered valuable, like diamonds and pearls. Perhaps there is some kind of chemical reaction going on inside that crater, something we do not as yet understand.

In the years since the loss of the *Gabriella*, two more ships have vanished trying to visit Nájar Crater. Other ships have experienced maelstroms, but none as big as the one the *Gabriella* encountered.

No matter how many warnings Ochoa Star Port issues, ships continue to travel to Madreperla, with the idea of mining Nájar Crater. Ochoa refuses to shut down travel altogether, theorizing that to do so would cause even more ships to go down, because they would see Nájar Crater as forbidden and therefore desirable.

No one at the Elizabeta Pub cares what Ochoa does at Nájar Crater. It is difficult to get any of the regulars to talk about Madreperla, the crater, or the *Gabriella*. Beta Linde walks away when the topic comes up, saying that she has wasted enough time already.

Belinda Pete spends most of her days in that back-corner booth where she last argued with Corey Burfet. She likes to believe he is still alive somewhere. She says it's possible that the *Gabriella* skimmed the surface of Madreperla, then peeled away, out of the view of the *Decker,* and traveled to a different sector. Maybe an unknown one.

"They're adventurers," she says, "and they all had trouble. Corey was in debt. Giles's family hated him. No one on that crew really belonged anywhere."

But she knows she's clinging to a thin hope. It's easier than thinking she pushed Corey to his death by making him take an extreme risk for money.

And she is wrong about one thing: Giles Ferguson's family does not hate him.

Every night before I go to bed, I touch the gold chains that Ferguson handed me for safekeeping the night before the *Gabriella* launched. It was rare for me to visit my father, especially before a launch, but I was a newly minted adult, just eighteen years old, and I believed I could bridge the gap that his travels and my parents' divorce had created in our family.

Maybe I could have, given time. But my father was a complicated man, not given to outward signs of emotion.

That morning, he would not let me go with him to the launch. He didn't even dignify his reasons by saying it was bad luck or not his tradition.

"I need to concentrate," he said bluntly, "and you'll just get in the way."

His last words to me were that he loved me and he would see me soon, but the last words I remember are that I would get in the way.

Maybe I did. Maybe my father, like Corey Burfet, felt money was more important than relationships. Or maybe my father felt that the money he earned on this venture would buy him back into relationships.

The night before he left, he removed the chain from his wrist and peeled the longer chain off his neck. He dropped them, still warm from his skin, into my outstretched hand, and then closed my fingers around it.

"In case I don't come back," he said. "You sell these. They're all the money I have in the world."

He has not come back. And I cannot sell them.

Every time I look at them, I wonder what his last minutes were like, when he knew he was going to die.

Did he think of us? Did he regret anything? Or was he fighting too hard to think of anything but survival?

I do not know. I will never know. But I wouldn't know the answer to that even if he had died in his bed, an old man with old regrets.

I tell myself that, but it makes no difference.

I thought perhaps writing this would make a difference, that I would learn what might have happened, how they all died or maybe, better, how they all lived.

But I cannot find that either. Only incomplete records of other people's adventures, their brushes with death, their experiences near Nájar Crater.

Imelda believes the crater itself is the villain. She tries not to feel guilty for refusing to go, but she is haunted by the crater. She is the one who led me to half the scholars I spoke to and to all of the scientists. She knows more about Nájar Crater than anyone else, and she has never even seen it from orbit.

But I do not see the crater as a villain. I don't see it as a live thing either. If the crater hadn't existed, something else would have snared my father. Or some other mistake would have brought down the *Gabriella*.

Her history is a series of mishaps followed by just enough success to keep her crew hungry and moving forward. Maybe that is the way of adventurers.

Maybe they all keep striving to find that one defining moment, not just the one that will make them rich, but that will make them spacer famous, living in the lore.

That is all I can give my father. A memory of the *Gabriella*, so she is not just one more ship that tussled with Nájar Crater and lost.

On my best days, I like to believe that the *Gabriella's* loss is but one step toward figuring out the secrets of the crater. On my worst, I believe the loss is all for nothing.

Most days, I think the truth lies somewhere in between.

I wrote this to search for answers, but I have found very few. All I know is that this project itself, old-fashioned and odd, is my adventure.

I couldn't stop working on it, even when I realized it would not give me the comfort I wanted. All the research in the world does not give me any answers and sometimes I feel like Belinda Pete, trapped in a past I'm not willing to let go of, even though I talk of the future.

I am not the kind of person who can step into my father's life. I am not daring nor am I able to captain any kind of vessel. The trips I have taken to work on this project—from my home on Ius Prime to Ochoa Star Port, on various ships that are similar to the ones I've described here, across land to visit different scholars in different cities and universities on the planet—they are almost too much adventure for me. And they are no more dangerous than a walk around my neighborhood.

I live in the realm of the imagination. Imelda asked me once, when I was deep in this project, if I was doing the work because my imagination failed me.

I wasn't sure how to answer her then, but I can answer her now.

I did this work because my imagination wasn't failing me at all. It was providing too many answers, too many scenarios. Each time I looked at the chains, I thought of different ways my father could have died. I imagined how his face looked in that moment when he realized he wouldn't escape the maelstrom. I imagined his body as it was being sucked into the vortex. I saw him being blown to bits.

I knew I had to narrow down the nightmares, see only the ones that were likely, not all the ones that were possible.

I have done that.

But now I know I will continue to be haunted by that last day, by the warmth of those chains as my father closed them into my hand, by his words, listing me as a potential distraction.

Maybe the answer I was received was to a different question. Maybe the question I had tried to answer all along was why he had left the family so long before the *Gabriella* launched a final time.

And maybe he told me, the morning after his big hand closed my smaller one, forcing the gold of the chains to bite into my fingers.

I need to concentrate, he said, *and you'll just get in the way*.

I was not in the way that day on Madreperla, and he still died. Maybe something else broke his concentration. Maybe someone else got in the way.

Or maybe his spacer's luck had just run out.

I will never know, and I am done searching.

Imelda tells me to put the chains away or sell them. I will not. They are my talisman, my touchstone, my reminder that we are all human, and none of us can see what our end will be.

But we will all face it alone, and no matter how we die, we will be the only ones who know what those last thoughts are, who they are of, and if they have any meaning.

Our survivors might be able to make an educated guess, but that is all it will be—a guess. A guess designed to make the survivor feel better, not designed to get at any truth.

This project is my truth, not my father's. Not the *Gabriella's*.

All we know for certain is that she is gone. She was last seen diving out of orbit toward Nájar Crater on Madreperla.

After that the record ceases.

After that, all certainty is lost.

Be the first to know!

Just sign up for the Kristine Kathryn Rusch newsletter,
and keep up with the latest news, releases
and so much more—even the occasional giveaway.

So, what are you waiting for?
To sign up go to kristinekathrynrusch.com.

But wait! There's more. Sign up for the WMG
Publishing newsletter, too, and get the latest news
and releases from all of the WMG authors and lines,
including Kristine Grayson, Kris Nelscott, Dean
Wesley Smith, *Fiction River: An Original Anthology
Magazine, Pulphouse Fiction Magazine, Smith's
Monthly,* and so much more.

To sign up, go to wmgpublishing.com.

ABOUT THE AUTHOR

New York Times bestselling author Kristine Kathryn Rusch writes in almost every genre. Generally, she uses her real name (Rusch) for most of her writing. Under that name, she publishes bestselling science fiction and fantasy, award-winning mysteries, acclaimed mainstream fiction, controversial nonfiction, and the occasional romance. Her novels have made bestseller lists around the world and her short fiction has appeared in eighteen best of the year collections. She has won more than twenty-five awards for her fiction, including the Hugo, *Le Prix Imaginales*, the *Asimov's* Readers Choice award, and the *Ellery Queen Mystery Magazine* Readers Choice Award.

To keep up with everything she does, go to kriswrites. com and sign up for her newsletter. To track her many pen names and series, see their individual websites (krisnelscott. com, kristinegrayson.com, retrievalartist.com, divingintothewreck.com, fictionriver.com, pulphousemagazine.com).

The Retrieval Artist Universe
(Reading Order)

Made in the USA
Middletown, DE
07 April 2021